Unspeakable Love

Barbara Timmell

contents

CHAPTER 1

The woman lifted her daughter off the boat and cast a final glance at the temporary home they had inhabited for half a month. Charlotte's experience had not been pleasant; being forced to travel in a confined space and unable to properly stretch her legs were considered a crime in her book. It was not by choice that Charlotte decided to trap herself with her daughter, Emily, in her humble four-wall room. The mere thought sent an unpleasant shiver down her body when she thought back to the crew's leering gaze, which perhaps could have been due to her foreign status or the fact she was the first female they had seen in weeks. Either way, this resulted in Charlotte wasting most of her time confined in her quarters, only going on deck to stretch her legs and appease Emily's curious nature about the different sea creatures she could identify when she wasn't throwing up.

Being her first time, Emily was super excited to travel on a boat like her father once did. However, a few days into their journey, Charlotte noted her daughter's initial excitement began to dwindle, and the only thing she desired was a pillow and blanket. The change in Emily's mood caused her mother to worry, especially when she started vomiting. If it weren't for the ship stopping to conduct a maintenance check, Charlotte would not have uncovered Emily's ailment was due to motion sickness.

Charlotte was astounded. Surely her daughter could not have inherited this from her late husband, James, as she would think this would be a strike against anyone who wanted to be a navy officer as they practically lived at sea.

As they made their way over a plank made of wood that acted as a bridge leading them to the docks, Charlotte was glad to finally put the boat behind her and be on sturdy ground. Although it would take an additional week to rid her nose of the awful smell of raw fish and seawater, she dreads to think about the humidity and the damages it may have caused to her hair. The thought caused her to run a white tulle gloved hand underneath her wide-brimmed straw cartwheel hat. A sigh of relief departs her lips, confirming that her frizzed hair was still sleek back in a bun.

She walks up to a crew member in charge of unloading the fresh produce the sailors caught during the weeks at sea. Pulling out their passes, Charlotte gives them to the worker, who accepts the ticket with a bow and hurries to retrieve their luggages. A few moments later, the worker returned with Charlotte's luggage placing it down near her leather-clad boots.

"Thank you...," Charlotte said, as she was reluctant to ask her next question, afraid the man would not be able to offer the relevant information. Giving him a once-over, she takes in his short build, dressed in a pair of loose linen trousers with his chest left bare to combat the heat of Twizhong, but in Charlotte's opinion it was just an opportunity to showcase his newly developed muscles acquired by the heavy lifting. His monolid eyes stared into hers, waiting on Charlotte's question, a feature she noted many people shared on the boat.

"Would you happen to know where I may hail a carriage?" she spoke slowly, hoping that he would at least understand one word in that sentence. But, instead, a pregnant pause stretched between them gradually, a frown marred his thick brow, and her heart sank.

"It's been a while since I've been on land," the slight widening of Charlotte's eyes indicated her surprise at hearing her native tongue in a foreign land. However, the soft timbre in his voice was soothing to the ear, and the patient he exhibits enunciating each English word. He pauses, scratching the non existed goatee while ransacking his brain before proceeding to answer.

"But, if I'm not mistaken, there is a carriage station straight over this bridge."

Thanking the crewman Charlotte collects her luggage from the ground with her daughter beside her; she begins to walk in the direction instructed, only to hear a voice calling out towards her. Pausing her steps, Charlotte turned back to see the crewman who had directed her, flaring his arms, trying to get her attention as he jogged towards her.

As he reached an appropriate talking distance not too close to alarm the startled woman and child, he asked, "Why don't I take you to the carriage station, hmm? Wouldn't want a pretty lady like yourself, ending up in the wrong parts of town." He grips one of Charlotte's luggage out of her hand and begins strolling at a leisure pace, leaving her with no choice but to follow.

After a moment of silence of them walking over the bridge together, Charlotte could no longer contain the questions she wanted to ask the kind man. "Where did you learn to speak the English language?"

"I spent a large amount of my time on the sea and have encountered a lot of English men throughout my travels, which led me to my two years stay in England. However, I met many unpleasant people during my time there." Charlotte knew the sort of unpleasantness he was referring to, racism. It was an unkept secret in England that everyone knew about, and only a handful participated in the game between the upper and lower classes. However, if you were unlucky enough to fall outside of these classes, even the lower class treated you as if you were the muck under their feet.

"I must apologise on behalf of my countrymen. But, unfortunately, though it might not seem like it, not all of us are like that." She stared into his eyes, hoping to convey how apologetic she felt about his ill treatment.

A sheepish smile made its way to his lips, "Milady, you should not be apologising on behalf of those mindless people." His eye strays to Emily and back to the mother. "You may have fared worst than I. There are many unpleasant people in this world." As those words left his lips no sooner, a finely dressed woman skirted past him, leaving a wide breach, fearing he may stain her silk frock-like skirt.

A busy street greets the end of the bridge. Charlotte leans to her right to address her daughter, "Emily, you must hold onto my hand, alright?" She grabs the child's hand, preparing to enter the chaos of the busy streets.

There must have been over a hundred people bustling around the market, shoving and pushing each other as they went along. There were a few instances where Charlotte had to use her luggage to part the crowd, not to say she escaped without being unscathed.

"It seems I, too, must apologise. Usually, it is not this busy, I'm afraid we might have arrived at a peak time." The man said as he kept turning his head to ensure Charlotte had not gotten lost in the crowd; any response she may have to his apology would have been futile. Spotting a space across the road, the man acted fast with his free hand; he grabbed Charlotte's arm and hurriedly pulled her across the street and into the vacated spot on the crowd's outskirt.

"It might be best for you to wait here until I can find a carriage." He puts down her luggage and hurries off, not waiting for the woman's reply. She wore a high lace collar blouse lightly embellished that was bloused loosely at the bodice. A leather belt secured her tucked-in white chiffon wrist-length blouse in her high-waisted skirt with the hemline grazing the street of Twizhong. Charlotte often favoured the versatile two-piece outfit instead of the dress; however, this did not mean she would not put on a dress now and then. The petticoat underneath the skirt aided the free-flowing movement and allowed Charlotte more mobility.

The corset underneath her two-piece lessens the pressure on the waistline by pushing Charlotte's chest forward and her hips back, giving her an S-curve shape. However, Charlotte supposes she must have looked out of place compared to the woman in Twizhong who wore dresses that disguised their figure with their overly puffy skirt.

"Mother, is this not exciting? We have finally arrived in the city." The nine-year-old enthusiasm was contagious, Emily's green-blue eyes flickering to the left and right, absorbing every detail the city had to offer. The two golden pigtails with a ribbon tied at the end holding the braid in place flared with each motion of Emily's head. The young child beamed into her mother's mahogany eyes and squeezed Charlotte's glove hand.

Her chubby cheeks stretched into a smile, revealing a single missing tooth, was just adorable. Charlotte's beautiful little girl. Emily is a Godsend, but her mother was keeping a secret unbeknown to the little girl. It is a secret that would wipe away the child's smile; just the thought alone caused Charlotte's right hand to grip her cotton skirt tightly, and it was at that very moment she vowed Emily would never find out.

Charlotte's late husband, James Wilson - God bless his soul, has always stuck by her side.

They've been trying to conceive for some time until Emily came along. James was her everything, the day that James first asked Charlotte to be his wife felt like yesterday instead of three measly years ago. Charlotte's lips slowly stretch into a smile as her pupils dilate with emotion, her eyes fill like a jug of water, her gaze lost in a memory of the past.

1856, how could she ever forget that year? The weather was bristling cold as though the Ice Queen sent her soldiers to terrorise the citizens of London. The trees were bare as though someone had deliberately separated the leaves from their lover's embrace; in hindsight, this forebodes the couple's short marriage. Shunned by his teammate - the friends he called brothers, the people he would not think twice in laying down his life to protect, exiles him for his choice to marry her. James hoped his friends would eventually come round to accepting his marriage, and yet Charlotte continue to stick by his side, but what did he receive in return? Threats from his family and promises of disownment, yet James did not care and followed through with his union by marrying this so-called uncivilised woman even if it meant he would lose everything.

She can still hear Mrs Wilson's obtuse voice ringing in her ear.

"You have ruined him! Do you hear me? Charlotte, you have ruined my son," the lady howls at the younger woman, quickly changing her approach, seeing that shouting wasn't getting through to Charlotte.

"Please, if you have any love towards my son, then let him go," she pleads, softly squeezing Charlotte's shoulders while slowly increasing her pressure after a few minutes without hearing the desired response. Then, finally, the older woman explodes, "You selfish girl! You call this love. You don't love him!" Mrs Wilson sneered as spit flew out her toxic mouth. Her grip on Charlotte's shoulders tightened, causing her hand to turn a ghastly pale colour.

"Isn't everyone selfish when love is involved?" Charlotte finally utters.

Despite it all, he stood by her side even when she begged him to end their relationship. His stubbornness was one of the traits she loved about him. But unfortunately, that trait was like a double edge sword.

It's a known fact in any relationship, there is always that feeling of holding that person back, and she was that weight sinking James to the bottom of the ocean. So many of their arguments stemmed from that issue, but he would not hear it. James was a kind and loving man that would take up your burdens along with his own, not uttering a word of complaint.

But she was no fool.

"Mother!" Emily shouted. Her voice sounded hoarse as if she had been calling out to her mother for some time. Charlotte's wide-brimmed cartwheel hat slightly moves as she lifts her head forward to stare into Emily's eyes, showing the child that her attention is solely on her.

"Look, the man is back." Emily points with her gloveless finger; the action causes the ruffle of her short puffy sleeve knee-length dress.

Charlotte looked in the direction her daughter told her to; with the crowd dispersing, she could see the man returning. A black stallion strolled behind the man pulling a two-wheel carriage. The carriage did not exhibit any extravagant designs but was caved from oak and painted a rich brown, making the carriage a lightweight form of transportation for a horse to pull.

"It took a while, but I have finally found a carriage." The crewman presents as the vehicle comes to a halt. A young man exits out of the transport, helping the mother and child into the passenger seat; cautiously, he guides them over the steps of the carriage, where a black leather padded seat greets them. Once both passengers are safely seated in the carriage, the young man closes the door and hoists himself back where he once sat.

Before the carriage can move on, the woman swiftly draws the curtain and pushes her head out the window, "Thank you for being kind. I know it's not much, but here," the woman said, taking a few shillings from a small compartment on her luggage and handed it to the helpful man. After the completion of the transaction, the carriage jolts forward, causing her to topple down in her seat as the horses find a steady trot leading her to the palace. With the curtain still drawn, Charlotte surveys the scenery beyond the window. In the world beyond her own, she saw the tired faces of people passing by as they whisked along to their destination.

In one corner, a store holder firmly stands while he markets away hair trinkets to an audience of women who seem too careless. At the same time, just a few feet away, another lost soul glares into the far distance selling jewellery. The women appear unwavering as their elegant silken skirt dress robed in bright colours change the tone of the atmosphere; their handmaids struggle in the background to catch up with their demands as they fumble back and forth to break ground.

One woman, in particular, aroused Charlotte's attention as her attire seemed to have been the epicentre of the small group. Maybe a fashion trend per-say, as at the hem of her bright skirt was a finely stitched golden pattern accentuating the roses that engrossed it. Her torso was wrapped perfectly by a dusty blue long-sleeved shirt that appeased her fair skin. Beautiful indeed, and Charlotte would see why all the other women around would want to dress just like her. With the flick of her wrist, the curtain flutters back in place, creating a barrier between Charlotte and the pedestrians.

Charlotte leans back in her seat, trying to find a comfortable spot as she shuts her eyes and enjoys the carriage ride leaving Emily to peer outside the window on her side of the carriage.

A/N: Like, Comment and Vote

CHAPTER 2

The repetitive clippety-clop sound of the horse's hooves staggering upon the pebbled ground comes to a complete stop as Charlotte's eyes wander to the driver for confirmation that they've arrived at their destination. Only to find two brooding jet-black eyes staring back at her.

"Here pa-lace," The driver states in broken English as he persistently points outside.

Charlotte's gaze cut away from his to stare outside of the window that displayed two pillars of walls stretching endlessly on opposite sides, coated in red. From afar, massive roofs shape into a broad rectangle. The roof's lower rims flare up to the Heavens in a unique curvature paying homage to a deity beyond the clouds, unlike the traditional rooftop seen in London.

"We are here, darling." Emily's head tilts away from her mother as Charlotte gently shakes her from time to time.

"...Mo-mother?"

"We have arrived at the palace," Charlotte informed. Once confirming the child had wiped away the sleep from her eyes, she leans forward and opens the carriage door.

Charlotte gazes in disbelief that she had made the trip from London to Twizhong, thinking about how this all came about by sheer luck. After James's ship went missing at sea and he was pronounced dead. Things became difficult. Well, as difficult as it can get for a single mother living in a society where a man is required if she wishes to be fed, clothed, and have a roof over her head. Let's not even mention the red target on Charlotte's back which society has taken great delight in giving her freely as if her appearance in this vague society was not enough. The predominantly obscure standard of beauty to what others portrayed was far beyond her own.

Four months ago.

The memory came vividly to her mind. She had been looking for work when Emily became ill. Charlotte had tried everything, but her daughter's fever would not break. Then, finally, voices began seeping through at her wits-end, criticising her role as a mother. She had driven her husband to his early grave, and now the universe had decided to take away their daughter as well.

She walked the streets of London aimlessly, trying to find a job or a doctor. Charlotte notices the pedestrian's eyes locking onto her profile; being the judge and jury of her social status, they whisper the atrocity of her crimes - a woman like herself walking alone at night was enough to get her condemned.

The sixth door she knocked on revealed a woman of Bangladesh descent. The wrinkles on her face indicated her age was between her mid-fifties or late sixties.

Charlotte became overwhelmed with emotion as tears began to cascade from her eyes like a deep wave.

"P-please, help me. Help my little girl, please."

The kind woman brings the mother and child into her house, providing the young lady a hot beverage to ward away the early morning chill. The older woman sits quietly, nodding appropriately between pauses Charlotte takes to feed her lungs with air before continuing her sentence. Then, having heard enough, the woman stands to her feet and introduces herself.

"You poor child. I can see you've been through a lot, but don't worry, you came to the right place. My name is Ananya, and my husband is a well-known doctor from India. I'll go fetch him."

In the weeks of staying with the older couple to initially monitor her daughter's recovery, Charlotte and Emily have become close with Ananya and Adi as they partake in their family meals.

One evening flicking through the newspaper in search of a job while she sat at the dinner table after a long uneventful day with no success finding a job, the presence of defeat hovered around Charlotte like a dark cloud on a rainy day. In the far distance, she hears a key rattling in the keyhole. A minute later, the door swings open as Adi comes bustling into the house after a long day visiting his patients.

"How was your visit with the Jones," Ananya asked, kissing her husband on the cheek, causing Emily to giggle at the sight.

"Mr and Mrs Jones are fine. However, I told Mr Jones to cut down on his sugar intake as it won't do him any good in the long run," he responded, placing his hat on the table in exchange for a knife and a fork.

"I passed by the market on Elm's Street with the Jones' maid in toe to pick up his prescription." After taking four bites of his rice Adi continues to speak, "I overheard a merchant talking about his three months stay in East Asia and that the Emperor is looking for a mentor."

In-between bites, Adi clears his throat; using the napkin resting on the table to wipe his mouth, he looks up, "Would this be of any interest to you, Charlotte?" he questions the woman sitting across the table from him.

"Yes, I would accept anything at this point, Mr Adi." She said with a defeated sigh.

"Well, that settles it. I will make the arrangements."

A/N: Like, Comment and Vote

Chapter 3

A group of maids identical dressed poised with elegance stood outside the palace gate, awaiting to greet the mother and daughter as they exited the carriage. Their colourful garments, made of lightweight material that would be considered scandalous by London standards, caught Charlotte's attention. Each maid stood in parallel lines behind a woman who appeared to be their leader. She emits authority from her extravagant hairstyle down to the colour of her silk robe.

"Welcome to the Twang Yi Dynasty. My name is Mei Lou, and I will be your guide."

"Thank you for coming out to greet us. I'm Charlotte, and this is my daughter, Emily." Charlotte shimmies Emily closer for introduction as Charlotte glances over to her luggage; meanwhile, in the background, the carriage assistant begins to unload her belongings.

Finally, the young lad approaches Mei Lou questioning her in his native tongue concerning the luggage at hand.

Mei Lou glanced to the side, sending a silent command as her entourage of maids swiftly moved into action.

"I think there has been a misunderstanding." Charlotte alerted seeing her possession being carried away. "The agreement was my accommodation be outside the palace; I am only here to inform the king of my arrival." A puzzled look sits on Charlotte's face as she takes a few hesitant steps toward Mei Lou.

"Not to worry." Mei Lou replied with a smirk paste on her lips as if to say she knew something that Charlotte did not. Mei Lou turns away from Charlotte, walking at a steady pace, making her way further into the palace, leaving the young woman with no choice but to follow.

The palace exterior is spectacular. Only walking for five, it was clear Charlotte was utterly immersed in the architectural design. Every twist and turn is carefully thought out, even down to the small details of the dragon busts elevated from the ground. The sheer sight took her breath away, leaving her in awe. The flooring outside held large ceramic pots that encompassed the massive courtyard,

A few guards were positioned in the massive courtyard as if they were defending a sacred ground with large decorative ceramic pots stationed on the squared floor.

Mei Lou leads them down a narrow walkway, emerging out of the passage into a-garden. Flowers of different species and colours were spread throughout, covering every inch of foliage it could find. Trees enrich in an emerald glow, with some growing tiny flower buds. Her eyes roamed the landscape and stopped at a willow tree, its trunk thick with age and raggedy bark that shared similar traits with the rest of the trees standing over six feet tall. The scenery was like a fairy tale taken out of the pages of Snow White.

"If you would wait here, a eunuch will take you inside the palace," Mei Lou suddenly stopped in her walk.

"I thought we were in the palace?"

"No, we are currently on palace grounds. Our first encounter was outside the palace gates, in the heart of the capital Twizhong." Charlotte's guide carried on, noticing the confusion on her face.

"Hmm...think of the palace like an onion in a square shape. As you know, an onion has many layers. The same is applied here."

"Do you mean to say there are different sections to the palace?" Charlotte questioned.

"Precisely, different wings in the palace are referred to as the 'south and west wing', etcetera." Mei Lou breaks her uniform stance to wave her wrist haphazardly in a repeated motion. "The eunuch will escort you to the inner palace where his majesty attends to the imperial court." After she confirmed Charlotte had gained somewhat of an understanding of the workings of the palace layout, Mei hurries off back to her duties.

"The garden here is beautiful and large enough to have a stroll, don't you think, Emily?"

"Hmmm, do you think we could have our lunches here as we did in the parks back in London?" The curiosity is evident in the young child's voice as she stares at her mother with a hopeful look.

"Well, I don't see why not." Charlotte spares the garden a second glance, absorbing its sheer size. So in tune with her surroundings, she did not hear the footsteps creeping behind her.

"Lady Wilson," a high-pitched voice calls.

A startled Charlotte clasped the gold locket around her neck. Her fingers toyed with the jewellery, trying to ease her racing heart before turning around to see a short man dressed in a silk maroon damask robe bowing to her. A thick white collar overlaps closely to the eunuch's long neck; as his robe flares to the side, two slits separate his garment, displaying black cotton pants. The eunuch carried a raven colour hat that shared similarities to a traditional samo that had small fans on either side of his head.

"Ah-you must be the eunuch that's supposed to take me to see the King. Please call me Charlotte. I am no longer married," she trailed off in a meek voice, looking down before passing a glance at Emily.

"If you will, Lady Charlotte." He said, making the necessary amendments as he gestured her down a different path she did not see as she entered the garden.

Charlotte exited the garden following behind the eunuch; each door was held open for them by low-rank servants.

The palace is magnificent.

Crimson and gold covered the entire hallway, and a mile of vibrant red carpet decorated the centre of the palace floor. The atmosphere emits power and wealth, two things the monarchy displays well. Small intricate designs covered the wallpaper, and on the walls hung scrolls high above ground depicting portraits of the past monarchs. Merely walking down the hall transported Charlotte into another dimension. If walls could talk, they would be like old ladies roaming the streets of London exchanging gossip like currency. Charlotte takes in the palace interior was enriched with history and secrets; anyone with eyes could see that.

Emily stumbles along with her mother hand in hand, their eyes feasting on their surroundings as they pass through different corridors. She is already off to see the King on her first day here.

A crooked smile briefly makes its way to Charlotte's lips.

Charlotte wondered whether or not she was taking things out of proportion. What is wrong with wanting to live a life of luxury, not having snobs look at you like they've just stepped in the trash?

Honestly, What's wrong with the King wanting us to stay in the palace? Again her eyes wander around. Charlotte finds herself reconsidering the notion of living outside of this jaw-dropping palace.

No.

She had lived in a society for far too long where men wheeled their power to wage wars and ruin a woman's integrity. She won't be crippled again.

"Mother, I'm scared." Distress oozed from Emily's voice.

Charlotte kneels to stare into her daughter's eyes, her skirt pooling around her stoop position. "Don't worry. I will take care of everything. Remember this, when you have blossomed into a beautiful young lady and have learned to make your own decisions. Never and I mean never, allow a man or a King to determine yours." She replied, standing back up and continuing with her walk, adding more determination to her steps. What felt like forever was merely five minutes when the eunuch stopped in front of a large gold double door.

"Wait here," he muttered before slipping through the doors and returning not a second later.

"I'm afraid the King is busy and is unable to accept an audience right now. However, you shall make arrangements tomorrow to see our King." He finished as if it were common for someone to be dismissed by the King.

His response chipped away the emotions Charlotte thought she had buried. They were emotions she felt she had left behind in London. The feelings of being overlooked were starting to creep in, and like the little mermaid, she was rendered voiceless amongst men. Charlotte had promised herself that she would not be that girl again.

"What do you mean tomorrow? And what if tomorrow comes and his Majesty is still busy?" She fired on without allowing the eunuch time to respond before carrying on with her argument. "So shall I come again tomorrow, the next day, or the day after that?" Inhaling and slowly exhaling the tension out of her chest. Charlotte positions her hands on her hips, settling in a comfortable stance, eyes beaming into the eunuch, preparing for an invisible battle.

Like air vigorously being pumped into a balloon, she finally snaps. "You listen here," growled Charlotte. "I am the King's guest, and if he cannot make my needs his priority, you can personally tell the King I will go back to where I came. Or you can kindly move out of my way and allow me to clear up this misunderstanding." Not waiting for a second, Charlotte marched passed him and in through the double doors.

A/N: Like, Comment and Vote

CHAPTER 4

A blast of heat greeted Charlotte's face as she stepped through the open door. The sight of red and gold walls emitted a majestic aura in the room. The colours entwined on the wall formed a passionate dance unknown to others. Carpet-like flags decorated the ceiling up ahead that dangled in the air. A vibrant long crimson carpet stretched out in the middle of the walkway.

Charlotte caught sight of an eight-metre long vertical gold scroll hung on four glided columns. The foreign calligraphy stood in the circumference of the raised dais. Behind the dais, a ray of sunlight pierced through the windows, causing the wall screen, dipped in gold, to glow. Mythical and none, mythological statues of creatures such as dragons and cranes, which seem to be from a children's book, stood in front of the throne.

She inhales the scented fragrance from the incense burners strategically positioned amongst these creatures, perhaps to ward away evil spirits. The statues differed from the drawings on the wall screen, yet, with each dip, the artist adds elegant swirls that Charlotte could barely make out through the sheer rustic blind, almost plunging the throne into darkness.

Court ministers stood on either side of the room, with the carpet acting as a division. Men clothed in green garments with their posture curved in, waiting to bow their heads if necessary. Momentarily distracted from the task at hand Charlotte briskly treads on the carpet like a map leading her to an unknown destination she follows.

If her presence was not already captivating, the echo of Charlotte's heels solidified their gaze; like a beacon, they honed in. The men in the room looked on with shocked expressions similar to how one would look at a woman entering a man's only club. The hastening of her steps causes the hem of her high-waisted skirt dress to throttle about between her legs with each passing second as she walks further into the room. Charlotte could sense their eyes imprinting themselves on her back. Yet, instead of cowering away, she marches on. The aggression is worn perfectly on her curvaceous frame as her straw cartwheel hat tips slightly to the side of her head, where her face unveils for the room to see.

Charlotte straightened her shoulders, turning around to meet their unblinking eyes. The muscles in her neck relaxed and straightened as she exhaled, steeling herself to speak.

"I need to speak with the king."

A look of astonishment paints the court minister's faces as their lips part like a fish out of water.

"I am the king's guest. I need to rectify a misunderstanding." A swarm of mutters break the silence as their eyes shift to each other to finally settle, looking past Charlotte's head.

"Misunderstanding, the King never misunderstands," a loud voice spoke from behind her. Charlotte turns around; her eyes travel up to the small staircase of the dais, tucked between the incense burner, to see a silhouette hidden behind a curtain of beads.

"We are all human. It is our nature to make mistakes. The king is no exception."

Charlotte must have struck a nerve as the silhouette behind the curtain paces back and forth. The tension is inevitable, with the only other movement being the breeze dancing between the beads. The voice boast, "The Heavens appoints the king; the king is no ordinary man and therefore does not make mistakes."

Whoever this man was, was beginning to ruffle Charlotte's feathers. "Does the King not bleed the same when we are injured? Does he not feel anger, pain, or sadness? If the answer is yes to one of these questions, then he is human, and humans are known for making mistakes. A title does not exempt a king from making mistakes."

"Insolence!"

A loud bang went off in the room, causing a cluster of knees to drop to the ground as the court minister's bodies collapsed into a deep bow. Their heads met the floor- not daring to look up in fear of being on the receiving end of the man's wrath.

"His Majesty, the King, please calm your anger," the men in the room all spoke together spontaneously. Charlotte stared at the ministers, her head turning back to see the sheer rustic blind drawn up, revealing the vexed man standing in front of the beaded curtains. Her eyes widened as realisation sets in, causing the only sentence to relapse in her mind, "Th-this man in front of me is the King."

A/N: Like, Comment and Vote

CHAPTER 5

Emily's hand squeezed her mother's, startling Charlotte from her temporary paralysis. She peered down at her daughter, forcing her gaze from the departing figure of the king's dragon robe. The sight of her daughter reminded Charlotte of her inability to withhold her tongue, and now it was the cause of their current predicament.

A cleared throat pierced the silent throne room drawing her attention to the slanted eyes of another eunuch, dressed in a rich robe with patterns elegantly sewn on. His attire foretold his high-rank position that aided his lavish lifestyle, wildly contrasting to the eunuch that greeted her in the garden.

He clearly hasn't missed a meal a day in his life.

He clears his throat again, causing Charlotte's beguiling eyes to cease her brief assessment and stare into the eunuch's kind brown eyes.

Suddenly, Charlotte breaks into a light jog, pulling her daughter along, having decoded the eunuch's subtle head nudge, indicating her to follow after the king. The short distance she covers brings her to the king's vicinity as she settles in a steady pace behind him.

She felt like a child. A reprimanded child, and the feeling that came with it would not vacate her stomach.

Charlotte knew she had to apologise, but the said apology would not leave her lips.

"I know an apology is required, but- "

The king slightly turns his head to peer down at Charlotte, "But?" he questions without breaking his stride as he turns into a corridor that leads them to the outskirts of palace grounds.

"I was unaware of your identity, and in hindsight, maybe my words were said a little too harshly -." Again Charlotte was interrupted, this time by the king's sudden decision to turn around and continue the conversation face to face.

"It is refreshing to hear one's unfiltered; a King does not hear that as often as he would like." His gaze swept over Emily before meeting Charlotte's eyes again. "However, it will do you well to remember that I am King, and my word here is the law." He resumes walking, this time at a much lazier pace, not giving Charlotte a chance to formulate a response.

After the tense moment had passed, he started to speak again, "I promised a home outside the palace walls. However, the circumstance surrounding this matter has changed. You must now reside in the palace while teaching my brother, Prince Syaoran." They continue to walk, passing by all levels of servants residing in the palace, each skirting out of the way to bow their heads, paying respects to their king. Finally, after a few more twists and turns, the king comes to a halt.

"You will work on palace grounds, and this is to be your residence." He gestures to the door behind him, "Your daughter, Emily, will join the Princess with her studies." His majesty announces having memorised the child's name from Charlotte's letters.

"Studies? What will I be studying?" Emily perks up, having heard her name.

The sound of the young girl's voice reminded the King of Emily's presence, lowering his gaze to meet her ocean eyes. "You will see, come tomorrow but until then; these are your servants." He points to the three ladies identically dressed, their hair woven in a fashionable yet modest style worn in Twizhong.

Charlotte stares at him, hardly listening to the conversation between her child and the king. Emily rattled off questions after questions. Once caught, it had always been difficult to contain her daughter's curious nature. The sound of a bumblebee could be heard in the distance, soft at first. Still, as the sound approaches rapidly, it is almost deafening, threatening to overtake Charlotte's mind, leaving behind a white noise. The haven of her mind allocated her time to digest the king's words.

Charlotte stood in shock.

No words dared to travel up her windpipe solely and vacate her lips. Not because she was scared, no-no, fear had long dissipated from her mind since learning this man's identity. However, this was entirely different, the confidence he extrudes while providing little to no detail as though he had time to prepare before she arrived. Speechless, she stood gawking at the king, piecing the clues back together to see the bigger picture. He was never allowing her to live outside the palace, and the presence of her carefully hand-picked servants was a clear indication.

She looked back at the servants, carefully plucked. All dressed in matching primary colour materials. Hand pose in front with a slight arch to their elbows, head tilted down, and eyes cast to the floor, waiting to execute a command at a moment's notice.

Seeing Charlotte's gaze, the king says, "They will assist you during your stay here in the capital, ensuring that your transition at the palace is easy." he offers after catching her watchful gaze while inspecting the maids.

"How gracious his majesty is to bless us with such kindness going far as to exert from his kingly duties to plan these wonders." The clip smile on Charlotte's face unwittingly told him that what he tried to hide unsuccessfully was already exposed.

"Well, if you would excuse us, your majesty." She bows and struts into her private residence, pushing the entrance door open only to see the front garden of the house separated by a walkway.

Two large trees stood parallel on the grass, tall enough to offer shade to those that decide to rest under their wing to enjoy a good book. As Charlotte nears her new home, she sees bright colours from the corner of her eye. She turns her head a little to the right only to see a few bluebells and white lilies planted with other flowers she could not identify.

Climbing up the steps, Charlotte suddenly felt the wind whip past her. She looked to see the cause of the commotion only to find her maids holding the door open, waiting for her to enter.

A/N: Like, Comment and Vote

CHAPTER 6

Charlotte felt uneasy with the servant's attentiveness as she looked at the one holding the door open, "There is no need for you to do that." Charlotte said, referring to the servant standing by the door waiting for her to enter the house.

"We are your servants, and you are the master of this house. We are here to serve, Lady Wilson." She responded, keeping the door wedge open.

"Please call me Charlotte. Mrs Wilson is, well - was my married name," Charlotte replies, confidently correcting for the second time. Her maids stare back with puzzling eyes as they observe quietly, "I am no longer married," Charlotte simplifies. The servants look at each other attentively, communicating through informal means with their eyes regarding the mistress before them; one bravely speaks.

"My name is Tai Ling." The young maid said, then pointing to the tallest maid holding the door, "This is Fai Min and Lou Lin," Tai Ling then gestured to the female with a medium build stature that stood next to Tai Ling. Tai Ling was youthful, as though she was no older than sixteen. The palace had not yet robbed the young girl of her energetic spirit. But unfortunately, Charlotte could not say the same about Fai Min and Lou Lin, as their innocence had left long ago, leaving a fortified mask in its wake.

"Tai Ling is such a beautiful name," Charlotte smiled at the young girl. "How old are you? And how did you learn English so well?"

"I am fifteen but soon to turn sixteen by next week." The girl rushed out, moving a little closer to Charlotte; at that moment, her youthfulness was much more present akin to a child.

"You are not the only foreigner to visit our land. There have been others before you. We have seen men with hair like the sun and eyes like the ocean, dressed in a black cloak with a cross around his neck, visiting, sharing their English knowledge."

"Do you mean the English language?"

"Yes, that's right. The king has instructed all new and old servants to learn the language before your arrival. Not too long ago, I finished my training after entering the palace and was fortunate to be picked to serve you." Tai Ling animatedly finished.

"Well, I am delighted to have you here with me." Charlotte grabbed Tai Ling's hand, adding a slight pressure, as she offered up a smile before walking into the house. At that moment, Charlotte knew she had already adopted the child, adding one more to the lot. Tai Ling was just too precious. She wondered what caused her to enter the palace; tucking the thought away, Charlotte entered the house.

The house was large and spacious, with dark wood floors laid throughout, giving the home a cosy feel. The open area reminded Charlotte of a living room furniture crafted from wood littered the space; placed in two parallel lines were six cushion top stools. Beside each seat rested a small side table, providing visitors with a place to rest their hot beverages. Above the step sat the host's armchair made from cushion stuffings with the colours gold and red fused, creating small flowers like a rose tree. A sizeable rectangle heavy cushion position at the back of the seat stops the user from getting back pains. Charlotte could see on either side of the armrest a side table decorated with ornaments with vases of different sizes and shapes.

Paper sheets lined the house wall; each wall held different paintings. For instance, the wall in the open area depicted clouds looking over newly bloomed cherry blossom trees. In contrast, the other wall had the brushstroke of a crane drinking from the pond. The artwork contained a lot of realism, as though one was standing right in front of you, especially the crane that was staring straight ahead.

"Charlotte?" Tay Lou called out, interrupting the woman's observation of the artwork on the wall.

"What did you say, Tay Lou?" The woman questioned, looking away from the wall.

"Would you and Emily like to look at your room?" Fai Min interrupted.

"Yes, that would be lovely," Charlotte replied, taking hold of her daughters' hand and following behind Fai Min to the next room.

They led Charlotte down a short corridor coming to a sudden stop; Fai Min stood outside an oval arch door that was arms-length apart. Windowless squares covered every inch of the door. The panels were lined with bamboo sticks, finishing off the look, a thin white paper sheet laid on top, acting as a mirrorless glass window. Lou Lin made her way to the front of the door as they both slid it open to reveal their sleeping quarters. The room was spacious.

The chosen decor made the room aura feel light and airy; even the furniture's deep nut-brown walk-in closet felt inviting.

The four-post double bed sat in the centre, creating additional space for Charlotte to add more furniture in the room if she wished. A light burnt orange silk draping hung above the bed's open ceiling. The shape reminded Charlotte almost of a carnival marquee she had taken Emily to see. The transparent silk fabric flared from the top as its body wrapped around the bed frames.

At the side of the room, Charlotte notices a moveable panel covered in oriental artwork, embodying the culture stitched on the three folded creases embedded in the frame. She was unwilling to ask her ladies about the item that had captured her attention and decided to figure out the object herself. Walking closer to the conundrum, she stuck her head behind the panel expecting to find the purpose of the furniture, only to come up empty.She was unwilling to ask her ladies about the item that had captured her attention and decided to figure out the object herself. Walking closer to the conundrum, she stuck her head behind the panel expecting to find the purpose of the furniture, only to come up empty.

On the far right side of the room was another set of doors like the one they had entered. Emily rushed past her mother, sliding the two doors open to see her living quarters. Her room was feminine; artwork of hibiscus flowers littered the wall. Walking further into the room, Charlotte spots a lignum vitae plant in the corner of Emily's bed. On the other side of the room, Charlotte could see a desk and a cushioned mat as a chair for Emily's personal use. She could already see her daughter sitting on the mat, around the desk, completing homework, given that she would be studying with the princess. Thin sheets of paper neatly piled on the table with a hand-carved oriental wooden paperweight rested on the left. On the other side of the table had thin writing brushes that differed from the quill pens used in England, resting against the inkstone.

A long stringed instrument sat in the corner, not far from the table, its weight supported by a Guzheng stand. The musical instrument reminded Charlotte of a portable piano or a zither, a large, rich brown slab of resonant soundboard made of paulownia wood sanded down to a smooth finish. Twenty one small strings like the ones on a violin, woven in a horizontal line. Unlike some instruments with fret space between two fret bars, this music board held none, but in its place had moveable bridges under each string.

"What is this called?" Charlotte nodded her head in the direction of the instrument.

"It is called a Guzheng with twenty-one moveable bridges underneath its strings. Females mostly play the Guzheng; however, there is a male instrument with a seven-string called a Guqin." Fai Min informed. Charlotte's eye swept over a final object in the room, another moveable panel with a similar pattern she had seen in her bedroom decorated with oriental design.

"What is the name of this moveable panel, as this was also in my room." Charlotte pointed at the furniture as she directed her question to Fai Min. She knew it would get on her nerves if she did not ask her maids.

"This is used as a changing room. If you wish to have a bath, lady Charlotte, we will prepare the room with all the necessities."

"No, that is quite alright, Lou Lin..., And where will you sleep? I did not see a spare room in the house?" Charlotte trailed off, looking around to see whether there was another door she had overlooked.

"Oh, don't worry, we are close by," Tai Ling inched closer to her mistress. "Our living quarters are next to the house to assist with anything you need." She excitedly grasped Charlotte's left arm as they headed back downstairs. But unfortunately, the moment was interrupted by someone speaking a foreign language outside Charlotte's new home.

"Your luggage has arrived." Fai Min looked at the other maids and began to speak in a foreign language. The language sounded similar to the one Charlotte had heard outside.

"Do you need any help?" Fai Min looked at her mistress as if she had grown a second head.

"There is no need. We will have your luggage brought into the house. If you would like to retire in your rooms." She lifted her arm in the air directing Charlotte back upstairs, where her room was. With a node, Charlotte retired into her room with her daughter in toe.

A/N: Like, Comment and Vote

CHAPTER 7

Half an hour later, having left Charlotte's residence, the King sat in his study looking over scrolls piled neatly on his work table, which he had yet to go through. His majesty did a quick sweep of the room interior, eyes settling on his library, housing books passed down from generation. The entire wall was covered in books from the ceiling to the floor, enriched in history. Picking up a second scroll from his table, he began to read. The ink blurred together as the character seemed to leap off the paper.

His mind would not focus. Instead, images of their interaction kept playing in his head - pictures of her.

Her features were striking.

Her physique was neither slim like the woman in the Twang Yi Dynasty but reasonably portioned that filled out nicely in her cotton long sleeve shirt and ankle-length skirt. Rich brown eyes stared with determination, her skin, some may describe as being a deep earth colour, like how the ground would look after a heavy pour of rain from the heavens. But not to him. To him, her skin reminded him of everything good, like the hot summer days when he spent most of his time as a child playing in the palace garden or the time he sat underneath the pink trees watching each petal dance in the wind. Or that time, he laughed with his grandmother, drinking rich iced tea.

Unknown to her, she had already caused a ripple in court. It was unheard of for a woman to enter the throne room while the King was still in session with his ministers; he knew they would have plenty to say about it. The mere thought caused his blood pressure to rise, dreading the next session at court with his ministers.

A sigh left his lips without his knowledge.

Their limited interaction told him much about her strong-willed persona, how she barged into court -fearless like a warrior charging onto the battlefield. Her heeled boots elevated her 5ft 5 stature causing Charlotte to tower over his minister's bowed posture on the ground; shoulders pushed back, head held tall.

She was...

Magnificent.

He exhaled again.

"She is going to be a handful."

"Pardon your majesty?" His head eunuch answered, reminding him that a King is never truly alone with his thoughts.

"Summon Prince Syaoran." The King announced. His eunuch bowed and turned to carry out the King's command but was suddenly interrupted by another presence.

"Brother, I am no longer a little wolf." Said the owner of the voice, making a subtle hint to the meaning of his name before stepping into the candle-lit room to reveal a youthful male face. His high bun sat loosely on his head, bound in a hair crown. Prince Syaoran's white robes hang haphazardly on his tall, lean build. His sharp monolid stared at his King.

Prince Syaoran's thick lashes aided his handsome appearance, giving off a slight feminine hue that hid his eyes from the harsh candle-lit room. His long lashes fan against high cheekbones, aiding the Prince's charms, which has caused much bickering in the King's harem surrounding Prince Syaoran's natural beauty, was a factor of his mixed heritage. He was perfect as far as the eye could see, from his straight nose to subtle plump pink lips.

"Careful brother, you wouldn't want to arouse suspicion of being an alpha." It was unknown to Prince Syaoran whether his brother - his

King, was merely jesting with him because if not, what he alluded to was treason punishable by death.

"My King mocks this little wolf. Your majesty has put this lone mutt on a pedal stool to sit amongst dragons."

The King dropped his scroll on the gold-coated desk, eyes lifting from the document he had been trying to read for the last five minutes to meet his own as if looking into the mirror itself.

"Why were you not at court today, Syaoran?" His majesty questioned, dropping the formalities and getting up from his seat to exit the room. The younger brother followed behind the eldest son like a duckling maintaining a respectful distance that demonstrated the hierarchy between them. Prince Syaoran took note of his brother's scarlet dragon robe made from the purest silk, the emblem on the garment was sown using gold threads to create four identical dragons enclosed in a large circle that foreshadowed the wearer's future. Like the emperors before him, Prince Syaoran bitterly thought, he too shall take his first and last breath in the palace, unable to leave this golden cage.

Prince Syaoran refocused his gaze on the king's robe, each dragon strategically placed; two sat on either shoulder, the third dragon covered the front of the robe, and the final dragon peered down at Prince Syaoran, five talons poise to attack or defend depending on its opponent. The mere sight brought about a memory of his past as a young boy sitting on the late King's lap, playing with the same robe that now clothed his older brother.

They made a sharp turn walking into the King's private dining room. Candles hung from the ceiling, casting the room in a dimly lit glow. On either side of the room stood an archaic fang-style vase that housed a small fire providing warmth for the inhabitant. King Long-wei made his way to a small oak brown dining table, directly choosing t seat facing the door they had entered.

"Does it matter, your grace? My presence cause rumour of climbing the ranks, even with your succession secured." Prince Syaoran drops down in the empty seat opposite the King as the maids file in, presenting a variety of side dishes on the table.

"How is Consort Shu? Her pregnancy is going smoothly, I hope. Your son will be here in a couple of months." Prince Syaoran poured the sweet wine into the King's cup and then his own, swallowing three gulps of the wine before resting his cup on the table.

"I have been too occupied sorting out the arrangements concerning the arrival of your mentor to visit Consort Shu." Prince Syaoran watched the King use his chopstick to clamp up a delicious dumpling bringing the delicacy to his mouth. Then, with his other hand, he picks up the cup containing the sweet wine to his lips, washing the doughy texture down.

"It has been too long," the King mutters, adding another dumpling to his mouth; not finished chewing the content in his mouth, he adds two more dumplings.

"What mentor are you referring to, brother?" asked Prince Syaoran as he gulped down the remaining liquid in his cup, tilting his head back and raising the cup above his mouth, ensuring he captured every drop. He placed the empty cup down and, with his other arm, stretched across the table to retrieve the wine flask intent on refilling their cups.

"No more, brother." said the King with his hand covering the mouth of his cup. "I am no longer in my twenties."

"Come on, King Longwei, don't be a bore. We haven't gotten through the bottle, and you have yet to tell me about this mentor." Prince Syaoran teased, tilting the bottle back and forth. King Longwei relents to his younger brother's wishes and removes his hand, preventing the alcohol from pouring into his cup. After securing his drink, Prince Syaoran settles back in his seat, finding a comfortable position as he cradles the alcoholic beverage to his chest with his legs dangling off the armrest.

Prince Syaoran watches on as his eldest brother sips on his drink. After two minutes passed, he then picked up the discarded chopsticks to cut a piece of crispy chicken.

"You will be finding out tomorrow. So why spoil the surprise until then, hmm?" King Longwei took another bite of his crispy chicken, reclining back in the chair to pick up his silk napkin to wipe the corner of his mouth.

"I cannot fathom why a mentor is needed unless this is some way to have my movements monitored." Sarcasm drips from Prince Syaoran's mouth as he turns his upper body towards his brother to observe the King's movement. Suddenly the King's right knuckle harshly bangs the table, with the silk napkin tightly gripped in his fist.

"Your majesty," The royal eunuch, the personal servant of King Longwei, steps forward. "Prince Syaoran's alcohol tolerance is weak, and he did not mean to offend. However, I am sure that in the excitement of accompanying the King, Prince Syaoran forgot to monitor his liquor intake."

"That is no excuse!" King Longwei roared, slammed his open palm against the oak table and stood up from his seat. The servants, including the eunuch, who had just spoken, bowed their heads in the face of the King's anger. "That does not offer him the right to lay accusation to his King."

The younger brother swiftly moved into action and kneeled on the floor in front of the King's table, his back arch into a bow, awaiting the verdict.

"Your majesty," the eunuch beseech. "calm your anger, my grace."

"Y-y-you!" King Longwei wags his index finger at his eunuch as his wrist trembled in rage. He walked from behind the table to stand in the centre of the room. "Hear my royal decree. Prince Syaoran cannot control his loose tongue and has offended his King. Therefore, as punishment, he will sustain from all alcoholic beverages for a month. During this time, he is to be confined at the temple to write a hundred scriptures on buddha's principles while he reflects."

"I am undeserving of your mercy, my King." Prince Syaoran thanked his King, not daring to lift his head from the bowed position until his brother vacated the room.

"Here you go, Prince Syaoran." The head eunuch handed the scroll containing the King's decree and exited the room to follow behind his majesty, leaving the younger brother on his own in a room suddenly deprived of warmth.

A/N: Like, Comment and Vote

CHAPTER 8

"What do you mean Prince Syaoran can not visit me?" Charlotte's eyes flicker from the novel she's been reading for the past hour, hoping the book would help the time fly by while she waited in the foyer.

The servant coward cursing his luck of being assigned the task of informing Prince Syaoran's teacher that her student would be absent yet again.

"Since my arrival, this is the fourth time Prince Syaoran has cancelled our meeting. And I have yet to receive a valid reason apart from 'he can not visit me today.' I will not stand for His Highness blatant disregard toward me. I am not leaving until I make the Prince acquaintance - preferably today." Charlotte lets out a slow stream of air through flared nostrils, her annoyance palpable as she not so gently rests the open book on her lap, giving the eunuch her undiverted attention.

As promised, Emily had started her session with the Princess; according to her daughter's admission, they were getting on well despite their differences. Without her daughter's presence, Charlotte was left feeling restless, not having much to do. Although Fei-Lou had tried her best to help combat her mistress's boredom, it was only so much Charlotte could take aimlessly wandering around the courtyard of her residence. And with a restless ward at hand, Fei-Lou's famous stoic mask was beginning to crack, allowing pent-up frustration to seep out towards an over-energetic Charlotte.

"That settles it. If Prince Syaoran can not visit me, I'll go to him." She concluded by getting up from the stool and dusting off invisible dust from her ankle-length navy skirt. Wanting to make an excellent first impression, Charlotte opted to wear a black linen outer coat. The gold embroidery on the coat collar descended into a small opening, resting above her bosom. Small gold metallic buttons were stitched on the front, which trailed down her torso. The garment separated at the last button, cascading into a downwards v-shape allowing Charlotte's navy skirt to be seen through the open slit.

"I'm afraid he is not allowed, visitors." The servant replied, not sure whether he could trust Charlotte to disclose that Prince Syaoran was being confined. Gossiping about the Royal family could get servants twenty lashes, but if they were unlucky to be caught, they would be brought to the torture chambers, strapped down and have their tongue removed; as further punishment, they would be booted from the palace. An unwarranted shiver ran down the eunuch's back; there was a much worse fate beyond the palace walls.

Charlotte could tell the servant was hiding something. Tiny beads of sweat gather in the eunuch's hairline like raindrops skating down the window pane. The sweat rolls down his temple and into his ink colour brows that had seen better days. His shifty charcoal eyes were unwilling to meet Charlotte's gaze.

He's nervous.

The telltale sights were evident.

"Alright," Charlotte inhaled and not a second later, she released the breath she had just swallowed and sharply closed the book she had been reading.

"The only way to get to the bottom of this is to see the dragon himself. If you will take me to the King." Charlotte responds, eager to escape the humid room. She brushed back the loose corkscrew curls that were not long enough to be braided down her back; a light sheen of sweat began forming at her temple. Charlotte pulls out a white handkerchief from under her long sleeves and gently dabs at her forehead before returning it to its hiding place.

The eunuch's eyes bugled, jaw-dropping to his silk robe chest; he was in awe of this woman's gull. 'Who does this woman think she is? No one just walts up to see the King, especially not a woman. There are rules that everyone residing in the palace must follow. Certain measures must be in hand when requesting to see the king. The gull on this woman! On th-this foreigner to merely think she can defy the order of things, she ought to be taught a lesson.' The eunuch's acid thoughts dared not slip through his paper-thin lips and let be known the grievance he had towards Charlotte as a smirk slithered on his face.

Charlotte stops in her tracks before exiting the door to look back at the eunuch, a dark look momentary slips over his face before vanishing with a blink of an eye, which made her question whether it was a trick of the light. An unsettled feeling made its presence known in Charlotte's stomach; there was a dark feeling that she couldn't shake.

"Are you not going to lead the way?" she questioned, which was all the momentum needed to stir the eunuch into action, rushing in front of her. Charlotte follows behind the servant as he leads her to the king's residence.

Charlotte trails behind the eunuch as he leads her down different corridors and exits. The palace atmosphere bustled with servants clothed in various colours that differentiate their ranks. Charlotte saw maids in pink robes sweeping the palace, whereas servants dressed in blue garments scurried around carrying platters of food. A ray of light bounced off a gold trinket, glittering in Charlotte's peripheral view. Turning more to the right to investigate the object, she spotted a gold hair ornament encircling the woman's head and dangled down the side of her narrow face. She was clad in expensive jewellery and robes that softly transitioned from a cobalt blue to a pale azure-coloured hanfu. Wrapped above the woman's small protruding stomach was a belt made from thick white flat cloth that complemented the streaks of white in her hanfu. The mysterious woman gripped a thin wooden stick; attached on the other end was a circular paper fan that she used to fan herself quaintly while strolling the palace.

"Who is that lady?" Charlotte questioned, taking note of the woman's entourage of servants diligently following behind their mistress.

The eunuch slows to a stop to look in the direction of what has caught Charlotte's gaze. "That is King Longwei's consort, consort Shu. She carries His Majesty's third son."

"I was not aware that the king had more children apart from the Princess," Charlotte focuses her attention on the servant, turning her head to the left, eager for the eunuch to elaborate.

"Consort Shu will give the king his first son. All his majesty other sons either died from sickness or were stillborn; with Buddha's blessing, Consort Shu will give King Longwei his first son." Suddenly the eunuch pushes Charlotte into a bow with her back bent forward as he, too, joins in the display of courtesy. A mere second goes by before the Consort approaches them, first passing by the eunuch only to stop abruptly in front of Charlotte.

A high tone pitch escapes the Consort's lips, words joining together in a foreign tongue. Consort Shu focused her eyes on Charlotte while directing her question to the eunuch. He raises his head to respond, "Greetings, Consort Shu. This is Charlotte, Prince Syaoran's new mentor." The eunuch greets, issuing the induction in English. Hearing her name, Charlotte straightens up, looking into the eyes that had been staring her down. "Errm ...Your Grace, have you forgotten his majesty ruling that everyone in the palace must use English in Charlott's presence?" He questioned, quickly taking the form of a lower now, knees kissing the ground; the eunuch began his explanation. "I mean no disrespect to Consort Shu by saying this, but the emperor will punish anyone who is found disobeying his ruling." He rushes to finish casting his gaze down, fearing that making direct eye contact will antagonise Consort Shu.

"And what if...no English I speak? " Consort Shu says in a jagged English accent, successfully putting on an act. Consort Shu knew all about the King's ruling two years ago-she was there when His Majesty orchestrated this bizarre idea that Prince Syaoran needed an English mentor. It wasn't enough that these vermins started tickling into their country to have one in their palace...w-where they slept, that's where she and the rest of the Ministers drew the line. While they shared the same end goal, their reasoning behind it was entirely different. The court officials were more worried that King Longwei had subliminally 'showed his hand' and intended to unofficial let Prince Syaoran ascend to the throne as the Crown Prince, seeing the King had yet to have more sons that weren't until Consort Shu fell pregnant. However, King Longwei would not be swayed. In retaliation to their outburst in court, His Majesty created an Imperial Decree stating all Palace members must learn to speak English in preparation for hosting the mentor.

Seeing that the eunuch wasn't going to answer Consort Shu's question, which further irritated her, sticking her nose up in the air and using her fan to shield half of her face, Consort Shu released a disgruntled 'hmm' and continued in a different direction as she hurried to travel through an open corridor with her maid's speeding up to accommodate their mistresses abrupt hasty steps. Once Consort Shu and her fleet of maids were out of view, Charlotte and the eunuch continued on their way, hastening their steps to ensure no more interruptions on their journey to see the King.

CHAPTER 9

King Longwei sat in the throne room listening to his ministers bicker back and forth, nowhere closer to solving the issue. In recent months the North Eastern province of Soreya has experienced a lot of floods due to the country's heavy rain in the summer. Since the freshly formed alliance with the smaller nation, His Majesty has been adamant about finding a solution to their problem. However, the task was proving difficult. As with each bridge they built, the infrastructure was no match for the strong current.

"Minister Bao, how many years since you've been a Ministry of Works, mhm?" The snare of the King's rhetorical question echoed in the throne room, forcing the ministers to cease their bickering and turn their bowed heads to face the Emperor. After a short pause, he added, "And yet it's been months and still no solution but a depleting treasury to show for your efforts." King Longwei's annoyance seeped through his pores, two bloody hours of listening to his minister's quarrel like children were enough to fracture Longwei's emotionless mask. It also didn't help that the Court meeting was moving quite sluggishly, adding to the King's mounting agitation.

He turns his gaze to meet the Ministry of Revenue, Official Hong, who is in charge of the Royal treasury, "How much is left of Bao's budget?" His Lordship's question filtered down to the other Ministers in the room and lingered in the air. Cheng He, the King's personal eunuch since childhood, scurried out from the shadows carrying in both hands a small pile of ledgers.

"Your Lordship, here are the ledgers from the Works Department." Cheng He handed the bookkeeping over to the King as he approached the dais in a submissive form. At first glance, the ledgers looked like a traditional book with two hardcovers at either end. However, unlike a conventional book, the ledger had no pages to turn but expanded apart like a slinky spring toy.

Clearing his throat Official Hong steps forward, "According to our records, Minister Bao has a balance of two thousand teals left." The King stretches for his reading glasses after securing the thin frame to rest on his noes; Longwei begins to scan the content of the ledgers.

The further his eyes read, the more his brows scrunched in confusion; with each ledger the Emperor picked up, his frown became more pronounced. "I am confused." The King finally utters, "It says here Ministry of Works spent sixty thousand teals, but their budget is only ten thousand teals. Where did this large sum of money appear from?"

His Lordship nonchalantly questioned the congregation, still yet to receive an answer in return. "Will you not provide your King with an answer, or do you think me a fool, Minister Bao?!" King Longwei's previous contrived calmness unhinges at the end as he flings the ledger from where he sat on top of his dais straight at his unsuspected target, like an arrow knocking the black samo hat off the government official's head. Minister Bao quickly kneels to the floor in the wake of the Emperor's fury, crawling forward instead of retreating as he wishes. The other Minister stood a safe distance in the face of His Excellency's umbrage, keeping their heads face to the floor and their hands clasped in front with their elbow jutting out, the extra material on their long-sleeved robe shielding their shaking hands, fearing they too would be caught in the crossfire of His Majesty's rage.

Standing up from his seat, King Longwei marched down his dais, and in four strides, he stood in front of Minister Bao, "There is an accountancy discrepancy in your books. What have you done with the sixty-eight thousand teals?" He stared down at his council like a sharpened sword ready to strike.

"I-I deserve death, Your Grace." Minister Bao spoke in an uncontrollable stutter, raising only to dip back down in a theatrical bow. "During the late Emperor rein, fifteen years ago at the battle of Mount Yeen, we lost one thousand men. Five hundred soldiers wounded in battle because of the war..." He trailed off, wetting his lips and directing his subsequent statement to the ground. King Longwei's patients were approaching an end as he waited for Minister Bao to explain how the war at Mount Yeen correlates to the unaccounted money.

"As a result, the deceased or injured soldiers could no longer support their families. The wives could no longer feed their children because no business would employ them, and those that did only earned so little," said Minister Bao. Gaining courage, he lifts his head, swallowing the frog lodged in his throat. "I was supposed to replace the money, but the issue with the city wall needed our urgent attention. Once the city wall was fix, other issues began arising and replacing the borrowed money became a distant memory."

"Where did you obtain this large sum?" He's serious now. Minister Bao can tell by the way King Longwei's voice steepens. Suddenly the Minister in question began to shake uncontrollably.

"The R-Royal treasury." Bao hid his head in the crease of his elbow, afraid to witness the fire in the Emperor's eye.

"Official Hong. Explain."

The Official in question rushed in front of the podium. "Your Lordship, I-I-I' am also unaware how Minister Bao borrowed this large sum without my knowledge." His answer poured out like an oasis. Official Hong flicked his eyes to the left, then to the right in the hope that if he peered long enough, the suspect would buckle under his harsh gaze. Yet none of the Ministers behind him dares look up or move an inch from their bow position on the floor. At his wits end, Official Hong racked his brain in the hope of stimulating semi-photographic memory of the past months, trying to pick out anything that he would now deem strange considering his predicament.

But nothing jumped out at him.

"What does the West say? Ah, yes. It appears the cat has captured your tongue." The King's arm shoots out like a cobra in the wild; his fingers sink into Official Hong's jaw, nails biting into his prey, causing Hong's head to jolt forward as they stare into each other eyes.

Instantly the room appeared darker, mirroring His Majesty's mood. "Guards! Escort Official Hong and Minister Bao to their residence." Hearing their Majesty's verbal decree, the guards outside the hall quickly entered the room, eager to carry out the King's command while almost removing the door off its hinges. The synchronise thundering of boots on wood flooring resonates in the room as each guard enters in a single line only to branch out and surround the suspects. The friction from the guard's movements caused their soft padded armour to rustle together while the red cape attached to their shoulder swished behind them. Left hand tightly gripped the hilt of their sword that still lay sheath in a leather holster at their side. The subtle action caused the room to erupt in murmurs; it was clear to the others in the room that Minister Bao and Official Hong did not have a choice, and if they decided to resist, their outcome would be bleak.

Before the guards could escort them out of the room, a brave Minister steps forward with the intent of advocating on their behalf. "Your Lordship," He starts, greeting his King by stretching his feeble arms forward; the smooth thin upright marble rectangle plack clasp in his bony hands offered up like an offering. His frail body moves around sluggishly, further emphasising his old age.

"Minister Lee, you are the most senior elder in this court. You have even served in my father's court." Longwei interrupts, "However, I am not my father, and this is my court." He looks around and directs his next message at the other members who would do well to listen, "If anyone wishes to speak against my ruling will share the same fate as these two and be put under house arrest until I decide your punishment." His Grace allowed a few minutes to pass, providing the next brave heart with the courage they needed to go against their King. When it seemed no one else would step forward, he returned to the throne and sat down.

"If there is nothing else, then you are dismissed." King Longwei removed his glasses and began to massage the bridge of his nose; already, he could feel a headache weaving across his temple.

"My King, we have yet to discuss Prince Syaoran's marital status. His Highness is now of age and is ready to be wed. I have garnered a catalogue of pictures containing possible suitress, which I deem a good match for the Prince despite his shortcomings. I have sent the catalogue to your residence, and it only needs your approval."

"Minister Song, your thoughtfulness shows no bounds. However, I'm afraid you have gone through all this trouble unnecessarily." The King visibly exhaled, allowing the man to sweat under his gaze. Minister Song is a short, stocky man, and despite his height, he is known for being a social climber. Lu Song's ancestor became the first General to hold two batons, and because of his merits, his great-grandfather went on to obtain a seat in court. In the past few centuries, the Song clan have grown ambitious, ensuring at least one clan member served as a Minister in each generation. However, it seems they have now set their eyes on new sights.

"Prince Syaoran is far from ready for marriage, and I am not ready to part from my sibling. He has yet to accomplish himself here at court; my hope in employing the foreign mentor is to aid Prince Syaoran to become a good Prince to the nation." King Longwei's response was clear and robust.

If His Majesty were a betting man, Longwei would bet his ties to the throne that Minister Song's daughter was among the catalogue of suitresses. Unlike other Ministers in the room, Minister Song didn't care about Prince Syaoran's 'short coming' as he puts it, and was still willing to marry off his daughter to a Prince whose mother was an immigrant who became a concubine if it meant the next generation of the Song clan would have ties to the throne, it was a sacrifice they were willing to make.

Before Minister Song could utter a word of persuasion, Chang He bangs the gon signalling the end of the meeting. One by one, they exit the room until the door slams shut behind the last person, "Sumon Prince Syaoran and bring us more of the fruit wine." King Longwei ordered as he used his left hand to massage his right shoulder, removing the extra tension that had accumulated during the meeting.

The Royal eunuch approaches the dais wearing a worried look on his face, "Your Grace, have you forgotten? Prince Syaoran is in confinement."

"It seems so." He chuckles, massaging his head with one hand. Slightly surprised, Longwei looks up to see Chang He is still there as if waiting to say something else, "What is it?"

"Charlotte has requested to see you, Your Grace."

CHAPTER 10

The eunuch who had prompted Charlotte to chase after the King was now leading her down a narrow corridor opposite the route she had taken. Recognising the servant Charlotte quickens her steps, eager to start a conversation with a familiar face.

"I don't think we had the chance to exchange pleasantries when we initially met. What's your name?" she questioned.

"That's because you were too busy being quarrelsome towards His Majesty." He responds in a clipped tone, unsure how to reply; Charlotte allows the awkward silence to fill the large space between them as she stumbles behind. A sudden shift in the air alerts her of another presence. As she continues walking, Charlotte catches the movement out of the corner of her eye belonging to the eunuch from earlier, lingering a few paces behind hers. Charlotte wondered why he hadn't departed, as he had already accompanied her to her destination, yet she flicked the thought away and proceeded with her next series of questions.

"This is not the way to the throne room." Charlotte looked at the Labyrinth garden they entered. The high edges trim to perfection; as they stepped further into the garden, she could see primly cut trees that were shaped into mythical creatures, trees tall as giants filled with every fruit imaginable.

"The King thought a change of scenery was in order after a stressful meeting with his council." They emerge onto a pathway leading straight ahead, not missing a beat, he added under his breath, "to alleviate further stress you will undoubtedly cause."

"What was that?" Charlotte swipes her head to the left, examining the eunuch's side profile with squinted eyes.

"I said, my name is Chang-He. I am the Emperor's eunuch," he responds with a grin showcasing oddly white teeth for a servant. As they got closer, Charlotte could make out a white antique round table that had a beautiful central flower motif with matching chairs. Sitting in the seat, the King sat staring into space dressed in his regal red robe with a giant gold dragon at the centre. As she got closer to the King, she noticed a gold square belt jutting out around his waist.

Charlotte supposed King Longwei was a handsome man despite his hair crown. There was an aura around him she couldn't deny, even now; the way he sat with his head resting between the clasp of his fingers, no one could deny his regal presence.

"Your Majesty." Charlotte greets with a courtesy, "I hope you are well?"

"Come, Come." King Longwei gets up, directing Charlotte to the empty chair across from his. "Take a seat. Tell me, how are you settling in?"

As they sat down, a maid approached the table to replace the luke-warm teapot with a freshly brewed one. Another servant hurried over with a silver tray gripped tightly in her hands. Stopping at the table, her dainty hands swiftly retrieved the tea cups from the tray she was carrying and set the table for the King's afternoon tea. The table was charged with vintage-inspired delicate bone china cups and saucers with different shades of blue dancing across the surface, weaving an intricate pattern.

"I am settling quite well, Your Majesty."

"Nonsense. I heard you've been quite restless these past days, even going far as pushing Fei-Lou to her breaking point." King Longwei's eyes perk up with that simple statement while concealing his smirk with a sip of tea.

"King Longwei, are you spying on me?"

A startling sound emits in the direction of King Longwei. He is choking. Surprised by Charlotte's statement, he released three chesty coughs to unlodge the tea from his throat. Charlotte was unaware of any birds in the garden until their chirping stopped. The servants froze, eyes glued to their Emperor, waiting to see his reaction; it was as if they were watching an intense game of go.

"Making such accusation, even in jest, can bring about immense consequence. Tell me, Charlotte, are you prepare to face the consequences?"

It was now Charlotte turn to clear her throat and look away from his intense gaze. She was uncertain how to respond, the man infront of her seem different to the person who often made it a duty to respond to all her letters even entertaining the mundane questions. A minute went by, and Longwei could see she'd become uncomfortable. Though Longwei enjoys ruffling Charlotte's feathers, it seems he has taken it too far and decided a change of subject was in order. "What do I owe such a visit?"

"I came to discuss Prince Syaoran," she paused momentarily, waiting for the servants to pour her tea. "He's not been attending my classes for several days. And each time I enquire about his absence, no one can tell me the reason." Charlotte releases her breath. Reaching out she grips the dainty handle on the tea cup and brings it to her lips, automatically closing her eyes once the hot liquid kisses her tongue.

"Prince Syaoran won't attend any of his sessions for a while."

"Why?" Snapping open her eyes, the alarm in Charlotte's voice was evident as she fired back, not giving the King time to finish his sentence.

"He is in confinement." He supplied, not giving too much away. It was as though they were playing tug of war, and she was beginning to become irritated with his short sentences.

"What do you mean confinement!" Charlotte voiced loudly, leaping out of her seat. "Your Majesty, with all due respect, when on earth were you going to tell me, hmm?" An aggregated Charlotte parrots on with her hands comfortably resting on slightly flared hips. Suddenly King Longwei's expression softened just a smudge, confirming Charlotte's suspicion; he had no intention of telling her - or at the very least, the idea did not cross his mind. Whether done deliberately or not, Charlotte was uncertain; however, she couldn't help feeling segregated, whether due to her foreign status or her womanly gene.

"How do you expect me to fulfil my duty as his teacher?"

"Prince Syaoran is in confinement because of his misdemeanour, and therefore I have postponed his sessions." Slowly he exits his seat to stand, "It will do you well to remember I am your King, and I will not stand for such tone, Miss Charlotte."

'Definitely, because she's a woman.' The thought floated across Charlotte's mind; instead of moving off course, she chose to file it away for a later date to be used.

"Will you also put me in confinement, Your Majesty, the same as you did your brother?" The simple question carried a heavy punch to her desired target. They stood neck to neck, eyes measuring each other up, both willing the other to look away first. "You may be the king of this land, but you have no power over me! "Charlotte's voice shrieks at the end.

Stepping a little closer, Longwei evaded her personal space until they were a hair width apart, breath mingling with each other. Charlotte was determined not to feel intimidated by his imposing frame, or his height he used it to his advantage to look down at her. Longwei once playful brown orbs now emitted frost as his face contorted in a scowl.

"Your Majesty," Chang-He called out to his King a second time, and finally, with success, his whispery loud voice penetrated Longwei's focus.

"What!" King Longwei guttural unleashing his anger on the innocent Chang-He, like a whip his head turn around however it was too late as his eyes connected with his servant. Before a fiery retort could be released, Longwei hone in on Chang-He's subtle message being told with his eyes. He was not alone. Taking in a cooling breath Longwei looks around spotting the kitchen servants lingering in the garden no longer with their eyes downcast but instead bearing witness to his and Charlotte's argument. The realisation finally dawn on him, how could he forget the number one rule growing up? Eyes and ears are everywhere in the palace, yet this woman has not been here a month and already she has gotten under his skin to the point where he had to be reminded by his eunuch.

"Leave." He spoke in a low icy voice with his back to the kitchen servants. Not wasting a moment they all rushed to leave until there were only two eunuchs left in the palace garden, King Longwei made his way back to his seat. "Be seated" He announced, "Charlotte, I will not repeat myself." Choosing to instead stare at the empty seat in front of him than meet the woman's gaze, not until he was sure his emotions were under control. Though she was reluctant, Charlotte heeded the King's command, slowly walking to her seat taking her sweet time in her last bid of defiance. A few minutes of silence went by, both refusing to relent until Charlotte released a sigh signalling her imaginary white flag.

"I beg of you whatever dispute you and your brother may have do not let it interfere with the purpose of my stay." She leans forward with her arms stretched resting on the table, hands interlocked. It was as if Charlotte was trying to establish skin ship to solidify her plea, but with a second thought decided against it. In response, he stares at her with a guarded expression, not saying anything for a while.

Also releasing a sigh of his own, "You are right. Prince Syaoran's punishment should not interfere with his lessons." Standing up King Longwei gaze flashed to Chang-He, "Announce my Imperial edict, Prince Syaoran is to be immediately released from confinement. Any future punishment shall not hinder Prince Syaoran's teaching with Miss Charlotte."

"As you wish your majesty." Chang-He responds with a deep bow.

CHAPTER 11

That evening Charlotte stood in a spacious kitchen that boasted a handful of slide-panel windows, which were left open to allow fumes from the cauldron to escape. Charlotte's familiar stubbornness was set and it would be a lie if Fai Min said she did not notice her mistress's show of reluctance to vacate the kitchen. Leaving Fai Min with no choice but to relent and direct the extra pair of hands to work, seeing that Lou Lin and Tai Ling have taken it upon themselves to entertain Emily until dinner.

Once she received a subtle nod of acceptance from Fai Min, Charlotte went and got a spare apron that hung in the corner of the room. She quickly tied the apron around her waist and got to work. A loud grunt followed by a thud drew Charlotte's attention to Fai Min heaving a large sack of rice off the ground and onto the counter, "You will be preparing the rice for tonight's dinner." Fai Min ordered before moving off to her station.

Charlotte picks up a wooden scope to gather the grains and pour them into a separate basin to wash. A few paces to her left, stood Fai Min, kneading away at the dough until it was one texture. Next, she retrieves a rolling pin off the counter and proceeded to flat out the dough, obtaining a delicate thinness.

"Charlotte, can you pass me a few of those carrots?" Fai Min tore her gaze away from her task and pointed with her flour cake finger to the pantry at the far end of the room.

"Sure," Following the direction given to her, Charlotte grabs the metal rings on each side and pulls open the pantry doors. Surprise to see shelves filled with vegetables, and even dried meat wrapped in tan paper, she stood too caught up in her thoughts that she didn't hear Fai Min approach until she saw a shadow of an arm stretch to retrieve the dried meat. Startled out of her thoughts she grab the carrots that were requested and laid them on the countertop where Fai Min now stood, back at her station.

"Here you are, Fai Min." Charlotte watches on as her head maid positions the knife in a chopping motion, cutting off the unwanted pieces of the carrot before skillfully using the tip of the blade to cut the carrot into thin slices to put in her meat dumplings while the larger pieces she moves to the side for later.

The sizzling of the pot and the crackling of the firewood drew Charlotte's attention over to the burning hearth that boiled the water in the large cauldron. Hearing the same sound, Fai Min waddled over to plop the dice carrots in the pot before returning to her station to get some seasoning to sprinkle in the cauldron. The burst of spices instantly coats the room, creating an aroma that brought up memories of a much younger Charlotte in her youth, helping her mother prepare dinner in their small house.She cast a quick gaze around her surroundings and once again took in the spacious kitchen, which was nowhere near the size of their own.

More memories begin seeping from her hippocampus, and one particular memory of Charlotte's mother came to the forefront of her mind. Charlotte's expression softened at the thought of her mother, the flood of emotions she felt blossoming like a butterfly being released from the amygdala in Charlotte's brain. She remembers her mother working as a maid in the kitchen for a rich family—well to her childish eyes, they were. There were days when her mother would sneak the eight-year-old into work, those days were always exciting spending time with her mother in the kitchen, helping to prepare meals especially when they made dessert and she got to lick the spoon at the end. But like a cloud, apprehension seem to always hover around little Charlotte, she feared her presence would someday get her mother in trouble.

"Charlotte? ... Charlotte?.. Have you finished washing the rice?" startled out of her trip to memory lane, she peered into Fai Min deep brown eyes taking a few minutes to register the question being asked.

"Oh, yes. It's all done." Charlotte said handing over the clean rice, having given the rice another quick wash. Taking the basin away, Fai Min poured out the excess water, next she took a handful of rice and releases it onto the bamboo leaf, and then she proceed to wrap the folds over the sticky grains. "I will be making rice soup," Fai Min offered up filling the room with idle chit-chat. Once she had covered all several balls of rice in bamboo leaves, she then place them in the boiling water to cook. "—For the sides, we will be eating fried dumplings." A comfortable silence settles over the room as Fai Min begins to make the meat and vegetable dumplings. Bending down to open the cupboard she retrieves a large wok and places it on the stove. Next, she picks up a bottle and drizzles the gold liquid in the pan, immediately the oil starts to sizzle and pop.

"The excess water the grains absorb will soften the rice and help it fry quickly." Fai Min said, using a wooden chopstick, she picks up bamboo-wrapped rice and place it into the pan to cook. She repeats the action several times and no sooner does the aroma of food and spices dance in the air.

"See, my company isn't so bad after all." Charlotte playfully bumps Fai Min who in return allowed a sliver of a smile to slip through. "I often remember helping my mother in the kitchen..., today brought back fond memories," she said, her tone reflective.

"Yes, I agree. It also reminds me of my time in the kitchen growing up." Fai Min utters resting her back on the counter, her mind drifting to a faraway place. A sudden sharp sound of a chair being scraped across the floor startled Fai Min from her thoughts, only to meet Charlotte's prodding gaze as she got comfortable on the chair. A puff of air vacates Fai Min's lips and with much reluctance she reveals, "I am the youngest and only daughter out of two siblings, learning culinary skills is key in becoming a good wife—this is taught to all girls, the only place they have in society is at home." Charlotte notices a mixture of emotions swirling in Fai Min's eyes, hurt being the prominent emotion. However, with an untrained eye, no one would tell the woman still held a smoke of defiance still breathing underneath the surface, with bated breath, Charlotte waits, expecting Fai Min to further elaborate but instead was met with disappointment. This shouldn't have come as a shock to Charlotte, unlike the other live-in servants, Fai Min had erected a wall that anything outside of a master and servant relationship was deemed unacceptable.

Yet.

These past few days Fai Min slowly began to open up, today is a testament to that.

Fai Min pursed her lips, eyes becoming serious as she held onto Charlotte's gaze, "I am aware things may be a little different in the West, but here we follow a system of hierarchy that has been around centuries, and just because someone wishes it, it will not merely reconstruct overnight." She stood up straight, eyes sharp —colder even as she spoke her next words, "Some people do not accept change easily, and will do anything to keep things the way they are, even if it means eliminating the threat." Those cryptic words settled over Charlotte's mind, and that evening as she sat around the dinner table eating the food that she had helped make while drowning out Emily's chatter at the table.

"Mother, today we found out that Princess Chwun and I will be learning the sword dance —puh-leaseeee say you will come to our rehearsal Mother?" The young girl asks stuffing her face with a rice ball, finding it too difficult to use a chopstick, and opting to use her fingers instead.

"Emily," Charlotte chastises. She grab the napkin off the table and proceeded to wipe the sticky residue from the rice off Emily's hands and then move to wipe her mouth. "This is not very ladylike of you darling. Lou Lin, please get Emily a wooden spoon."

Charlotte lightly shook her head in jest, she didn't understand how her daughter could be such a messy eater. But she guess that came with the territory of being a parent to a nine-year-old with boyish characteristics. Charlotte tried not to be too critical of Emily and her lack of etiquette. However, the mother was too aware of raising a child that society was against her having and what made matters worst were the comments.

'How can a monkey teach one of our own etiquettes?'

'She will only turn the child into an uncivilised beast.'

"Mother...M-mother! Stop it already, anymore and I think you might succeed in wiping off my lips." Emily cheekily said around the thick napkin causing a muffled chuckle amongst the servants

"Sorry, dear." Charlotte said gently pinching Emily's cheek, "So, what is this about sword dancing? I don't know how to feel about you playing with swords, a sword is no game you could get hurt, Emily."

Before Emily could respond, Lou Lin return to the table catching the young girl taking a hefty bite from her third rice ball, seeing Emily try to quickly finish the excess food in her mouth. Lou Lin quietly place the wooden spoon next to the child's plate and made her way to her seat opposite the mother.

"Thank you, Lou Lin." Emily quickly muttered causing a few rice grains to fly across the table, after receiving a sharp look from Charlotte. Lou Lin accepts the child's appreciation and gave a nod in return before picking up her chopsticks to eat her meal.

"Mother, we don't use real swords silly, according to our dance teacher we will be using a Sakura tree. Princess Chwun said we get to wear beautiful dresses when we perform the sword dance. Mother, won't you come and watch us on Friday, pleasseee." The young girl dramatically begs as she turns to face her mother. It was clear that anything to do with putting on a pretty dress or getting all dressed up was something that Emily thoroughly enjoyed and didn't need much persuading.

A sudden sharp knock interrupted Charlotte's response, causing everyone around the table to pause. As they sat in silence none dare speak instead they chose to exchange worried glances and questionable looks to who could be visiting at this hour. The knock sounded again, this time a lot harsher, seeing that no one was willing to get up Fai Min decided to be the one to investigate.

"Who is it?" Charlotte questioned as she heard the twist of the handle which was followed by a creak signalling the door opening. A small muttering back and forth between Fai Min and the stranger before she came back into view.

"A eunuch?... is requesting your presence."

Charlotte gets up from her chair and heads over to the door with Fai Min closely behind. "Oh—it's you" Charlotte voice seeing the familiar face of the eunuch who was sent to inform her of Prince Syaoran's absence.

"Prince Syaoran has requested your presence."

Charlotte almost didn't hear him over the thunder that sounded outside. "It's late, why would he request to see me at this hour?" She gaze at him in puzzlement as another flash lightning bolt lit up the sky lasting a little over a minute. The brief bolt of light enable Charlotte to assess her surroundings, taking note of the mist and lack of stars in the night, she guess she was in the kitchen longer than she thought.

"It has come to Prince Syaoran's attention that you aided him with his early release, and so he wishes to personally thank you."

"There is no need. I simply spoke to the King about Prince Syaoran's confinement and how it was interfering with his lessons."

He steps forward eating away the distance between them. "You don't seem to fathom the importance of what you accomplish today. It takes others years to obtain, however, you were able to achieve in a day." The eunuch peered down his nose at Charlotte and his next words were said slowly as if she was a simp. "Having the King's ear is no trivial matter, think of the palace like a dangerous Arena and the King is your weapon."

A silent sigh left Charlotte's plum lips, "Thank you for that interesting analogy I will keep that in mind."

Sensing a shadow behind her, Charlotte turns to see Fai Min, "This shouldn't take long, please put Emily to bed in ten minutes." Charlotte quickly picks an umbrella from the pile next to the door as she had yet to change out of her dress from this morning.

Making her outside where she left the eunuch waiting."After you." As the door slammed shut no longer giving the woman a choice to turn back. Charlotte followed the eunuch with Fai Min's words still racing in her mind.

CHAPTER 12

In a dark-lit room, an unconscious man lay in a single cot. Small bead-like sweat gathered in his hairline merging like a stream, trickling down his temple and into his overgrown beard.

The man's face contorted in pain, soft groans slip past beard cover lips. The room held little to no furniture. The smoke from the incense weaves through the space between furniture drifting to the ceiling to form a pillow of clouds. A door creaks open followed by small feet. The intruder crosses the entrance of the doorway, to then pause. Before silence could completely engulf the room, the sudden sound of bare feet slapping on the hard floor restarted again, this time with more haste, going further in the room until abruptly stopping in front of the bed. The young child eagerly pushes his dark strands out of his slanted eyes to get a better look at the mysterious stranger.

The man's skin once held a pinkish hue now became a dull grey, sparking the child's curiosity. Plucking the courage, the boy wrapped his small hand around the man's cold finger and pulled. A short burst of giggles escapes from the child's balloon-like cheeks as the man contorts in pain, suddenly realising his mistake the boy quickly slaps his hands over his mouth, causing the remainder of the laugh to be muffled.

"Pi Yu!" A woman shrill in the distance. "I hope you are not in that room again causing mischief" Hearing the reprimand in his mother's voice and the heavy footsteps that followed, the child sprinted out of the room as fast as his little feet could take him screaming along the way, "The man is crying, Mama!"

The adult quickens her steps, finding the child's response alarming, she barges through the door and with three long strides she stands at his cot.

"My goodness!" As if burnt, she quickly withdraws her hand from the man's head."He is not crying, he is burning up. Pi Yu! Fetch me a basin of cold water and a cloth." She begins unbuttoning his shirt. Her action went against all etiquette taught amongst women.

It has been over two years since she found him washed up on shore barely alive. Though she could not afford another mouth to feed her conscious would not allow her to leave the poor soul for dead.

She wondered what atrocity life dealt him to end up this way. Her atrocity was the war in Mount Yeen that stole her joy and left her life in ruins. After the battle, the troops arrived home not exactly drunk on the high that comes from defeating your enemy in an intense battle.

Instead, they returned empty.

Their eyes were vacant as though these men were still reliving the events that took place on the battlefield, seeing their comrades take their last breath, the thought alone sent chills down her back.

Her husband was not left unscathed either, he too wore terrors of war on his body that eventually ate away at his former self, leading him to find solace at the end of a bottle. He couldn't fathom that he no longer had an able body, many men who had made the gruelling trip back home from their victory were left disabled. It took six months. Six months for him to give up on life and for the alcohol to finally catch up to him.

Pi Yu returned with the basin, slushing the water in the process and startling his mother from her reverie. Seeing the boy struggle the mother hurried forward taking the heavy basin and placing it by the bed. She picked up the cloth allowing the material to be emerg under water, squeezing the excess liquid she applied the wet cloth to the man's forehead her touch lingered in its journey as she marvelled in the texture of his honey locks — which hadn't seen a comb over a month.

After her husband's death, her world came crashing down in the form of two burly men claiming her husband had signed their home away as collateral damage — in case he fell behind paying off his gambling debt. She had no husband. No source of income. No home, she had hit rock bottom.

If it weren't for Minister Bao's generosity they —she wouldn't have survived up to this point. He ensured that all those heavily affected by the war received compensation. Even offering more to widows and wives who became the main breadwinners because of their husband's disability. The compensation she received from Bao contributed tremendously to her survival in the coming six months, eventually, she found employment working on the seashore.

The man violently tossed his head back and forth as if locked in a bad dream. The sudden movement captures the woman's attention causing her to repeat the action by rinsing the cloth, but instead, she cleans his face in hopes the cool water would give some comfort.

In response he grits his teeth, struggling with an invisible pain. His mumbling was like a chant at first inaudible but as it progressed the mumble got louder and his words got clearer.

"Ch..ar.."

"Char...lotte"